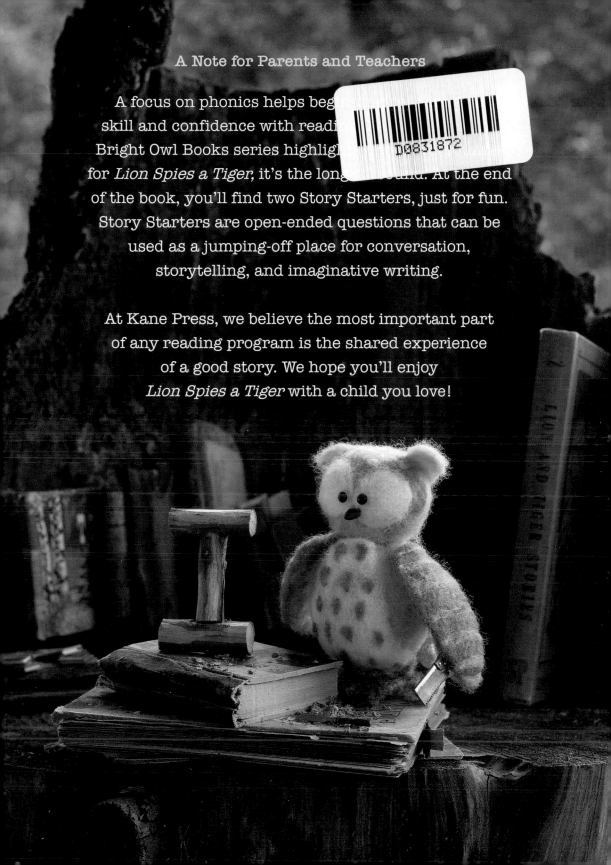

A Note for Parents and Teachers

A focus on phonics helps beg[...]
skill and confidence with readi[...]
Bright Owl Books series highlig[...]
for *Lion Spies a Tiger*, it's the long [...] sound. At the end
of the book, you'll find two Story Starters, just for fun.
Story Starters are open-ended questions that can be
used as a jumping-off place for conversation,
storytelling, and imaginative writing.

At Kane Press, we believe the most important part
of any reading program is the shared experience
of a good story. We hope you'll enjoy
Lion Spies a Tiger with a child you love!

Library of Congress Cataloging-in-Publication Data
Names: Coxe, Molly, author, illustrator.
Title: Lion spies a tiger / by Molly Coxe.
Description: New York : Kane Press, [2019] | Series: Bright Owl books |
Summary: Lion sets out to show his friend Spike how good his eyesight is, even at night, but learns he was mistaken.
Identifiers: LCCN 2018024729 (print) | LCCN 2018030517 (ebook) | ISBN 9781635921083 (ebook) | ISBN 9781635921076 (pbk.) | ISBN 9781635921069 (reinforced library binding)
Subjects: | CYAC: Vision—Fiction. | Eyeglasses—Fiction. | Lions—Fiction.
Classification: LCC PZ7.C839424 (ebook) | LCC PZ7.C839424 Lio 2019 (print) | DDC [E]—dc23
LC record available at https://lccn.loc.gov/2018024729

10 9 8 7 6 5 4 3 2 1

First published in the United States of America in 2019 by Kane Press, Inc.
Printed in China

Book Design: Michelle Martinez

Bright Owl Books is a registered trademark of Kane Press, Inc.

Visit us online at www.kanepress.com

 Like us on Facebook
facebook.com/kanepress

 Follow us on Twitter
@KanePress

Lion Spies a Tiger

by **Molly Coxe**

LIBRARY →

Kane Press • New York

Lion and Spike
are at the library.
"Lions can see for miles,"
Lion reads.
"Even at night?"
asks Spike.

"Even at night,"
says Lion.
"Climb on.
I'll give it a try."

Spike climbs on.
Lion glides
through the night.
"I spy bright stars
in the sky,"
says Lion.

"Those aren't bright stars
 in the sky.
 Those are fireflies!"
 says Spike.
 "Try again."

Lion climbs up high.
He says,
"I spy city lights."

"Those aren't city lights,"
says Spike.
"That's a sign for pizza pie!
Try again."

Lion lies down
by a tall pine.
He says,
"I spy two eyes
and five stripes."

"Yikes!" cries Lion. "I spy **A TIGER!**"

Lion fights the tiger.
Lion bites the tiger.
All night,
Lion fights and bites.

Finally, it is light.
"Where is the tiger?"
asks Lion.

"The tiger was not a tiger,"
says Spike.
"It was a kite."

Lion sighs.
He says,
"I cannot see for miles.
I cannot see at night.
I am not a lion!"

"Of course you are a lion,"
says Spike.
"I have an idea.
Let's see Dr. Rhino."

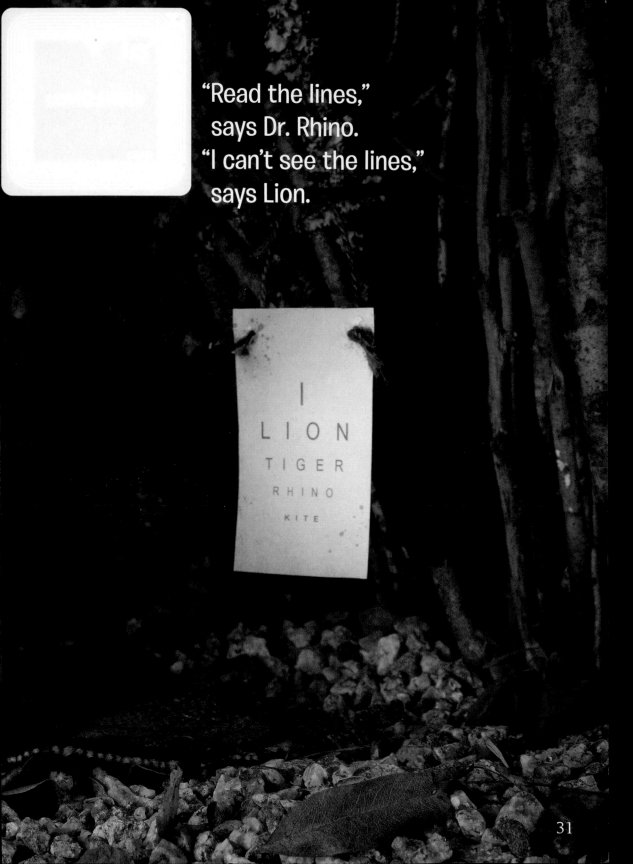

"Read the lines,"
 says Dr. Rhino.
"I can't see the lines,"
 says Lion.

I

LION

TIGER

RHINO

KITE

"Now try," says Dr. Rhino.
"L, I, O, N,
T, I, G, E, R,
R, H, I, N, O,
K, I, T, E,"
says Lion.
"Right!" says Dr. Rhino.

"Try these," says Dr. Rhino.
"You look nice!" says Spike.

Lion can see for miles
even at night.
"I spy fireflies,
a sign for pizza pie,
and my friend, Spike,
by my side!" says Lion.

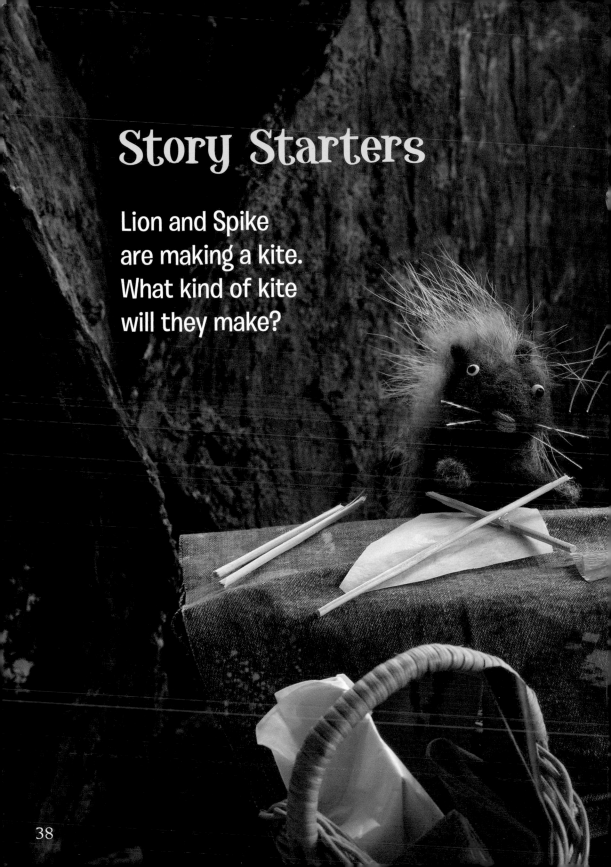

Story Starters

Lion and Spike
are making a kite.
What kind of kite
will they make?

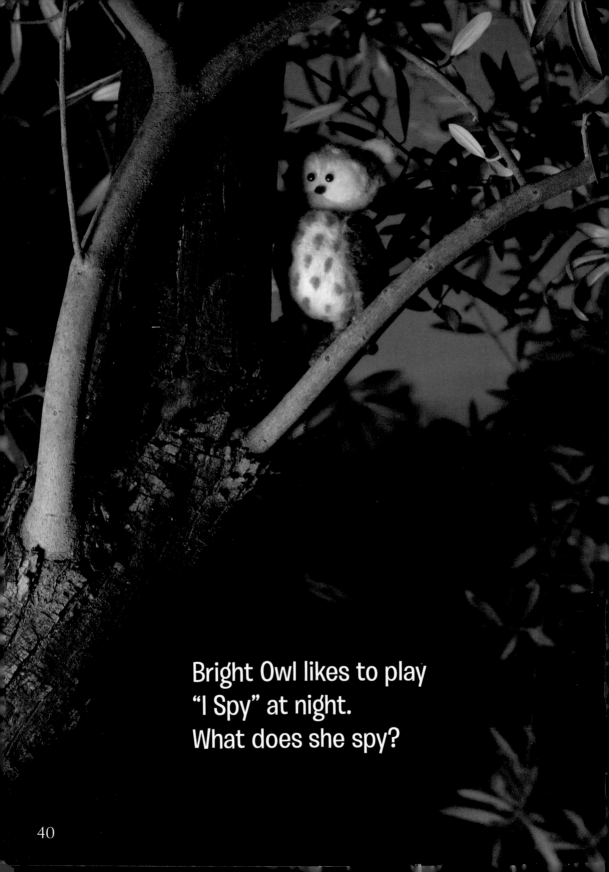

Bright Owl likes to play
"I Spy" at night.
What does she spy?